For my boys –
Adam, Guy and Ollie

First published 2017 by Nosy Crow Ltd
The Crow's Nest, Baden Place, Crosby Row, London, SE11YW
www.nosycrow.com

ISBN 978 0 85763 858 8

Nosy Crow and associated logos are trademarks
and/or registered trademarks of Nosy Crow Ltd.

A CIP catalogue reord for this book is available from the British Library.

Printed in China by Imago

Papers used by Nosy Crow are made from wood grown in sustainable forests.

10 9 8 7 6 5 4 3 2 1

Stick!

Irene Dickson

Find a stick,

a very useful stick.

Walk with it.

Throw it.

Tap it.

Balance with it.

Swish it.

Draw with it.

Stir with it.

Throw it again.

Wave it.

Be careful!

Don't drop it!

See it fall . . .

. . . watch it float.

Find a stick . . .

. . . a very useful stick.